A Mouse in the House

First published 2007
Evans Brothers Limited
2A Portman Mansions
Chiltern St
London W1U 6NR

British Library Cataloguing in Publication Data
French, Vivian
        A mouse in the house. - (Zig zag)
        1. Children's stories
        I. Title
        823.9'14[J]

ISBN-10: 0 237 53163 1 (hb)
13 digit ISBN: 978 0237 53163 8
ISBN-10: 0 237 53167 4 (pb)
13 digit ISBN: 978 0237 53167 6

Printed in China

Series Editor: Nick Turpin
Design: Robert Walster
Production: Jenny Mulvanny

A Mouse in the House

by Vivian French

illustrated by Tim Archbold

Evans

"Somebody help me,
help me, please…

There's a mouse in
my house…

…and it's eating my cheese!"

8

"Never mind, Gran — I've a cure for that. What you need is a black and white CAT!"

Where DID that cat go?

All that I've got today
in my house is a...

"Don't worry, Gran, I know what to do. A big spotty DOG is the thing for you!"

Where DID that dog go?

All that I've got today
in my house…

…is a big and spotty
black and white mouse!"

"Don't worry Gran,
I know what to do…

...a dear little FLEA
is the thing for you."

"Three cheers! That mouse
has scurried away.

There's only ME in my house today..."

"Somebody help me!
Help me, please –

I'm itching and scratching...

Why not try reading another ZigZag book?

Dinosaur Planet
by David Orme and Fabiano Fiorin
ISBN 0 237 52667 0

Tall Tilly
by Jillian Powell and Tim Archbold
ISBN 0 237 52668 9

Batty Betty's Spells
by Hilary Robinson and Belinda Worsley
ISBN 0 237 52669 7

The Thirsty Moose
by David Orme and Mike Gordon
ISBN 0 237 52666 2

The Clumsy Cow
by Julia Moffat and Lisa Williams
ISBN 0 237 52656 5

Open Wide!
by Julia Moffatt and Anni Axworthy
ISBN 0 237 52657 3

Too Small
by Kay Woodward and Deborah van de Leigraaf
ISBN 0 237 52777 4

I Wish I Was An Alien
by Vivian French and Lisa Williams
ISBN 0 237 52776 6

The Disappearing Cheese
by Paul Harrison and Ruth Rivers
ISBN 0 237 52775 8

Terry the Flying Turtle
by Anna Wilson and Mike Gordon
ISBN 0 237 52774 X

Pet To School Day
by Hilary Robinson and Tim Archbold
ISBN 0 237 52773 1

The Cat in the Coat
by Vivian French and Alison Bartlett
ISBN 0 237 52772 3

Pig in Love
by Vivian French and Tim Archbold
ISBN 0 237 52950 5

The Donkey That Was Too Fast
by David Orme and Ruth Rivers
ISBN 0 237 52949 1

The Yellow Balloon
by Helen Bird and Simona Dimitri
ISBN 0 237 52948 3

Hamish Finds Himself
by Jillian Powell and Belinda Worsley
ISBN 0 237 52947 5

Flying South
by Alan Durant and Kath Lucas
ISBN 0 237 52946 7

Croc by the Rock
by Hilary Robinson and Mike Gordon
ISBN 0 237 52945 9

Turn off the Telly!
by Charlie Gardner and Barbara Nascimbeni
ISBN 0 237 53168 2

Fred and Finn
by Madeline Goodey and Mike Gordon
ISBN 0 237 53169 0

A Mouse in the House
by Vivian French and Tim Archbold
ISBN 0 237 53167 4

Lovely, Lovely Pirate Gold
by Scoular Anderson
ISBN 0 237 53170 4